KERMIT & CLEOPIGTRA

Starring

Jim Henson's Muppets™

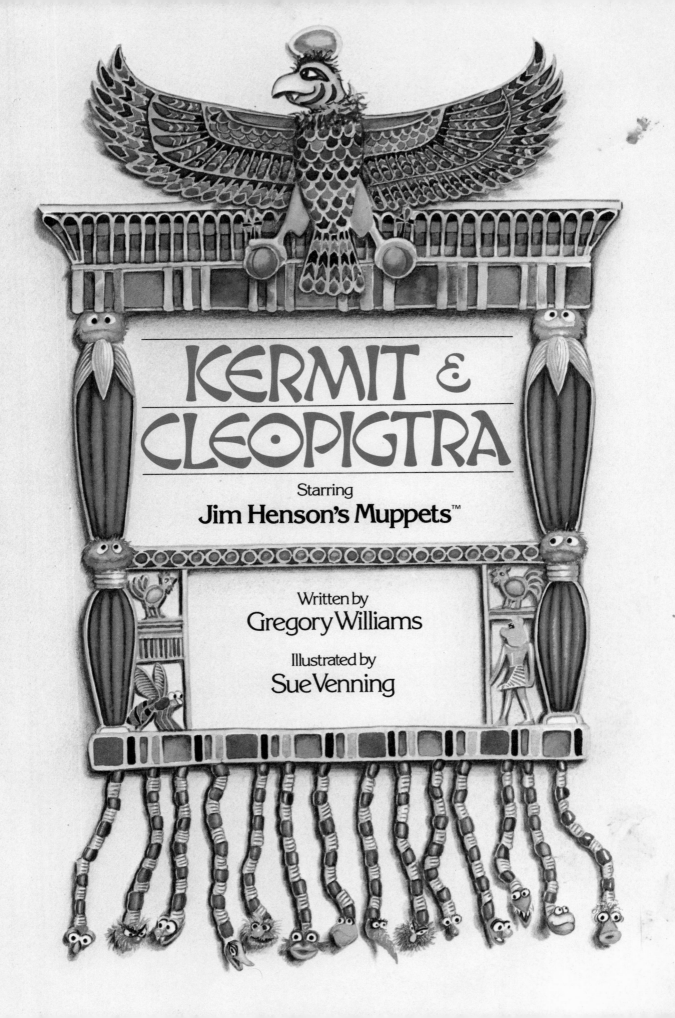

KERMIT &
CLEOPIGTRA

Starring
Jim Henson's Muppets™

Written by
Gregory Williams

Illustrated by
Sue Venning

CHAPTER ONE

"That's it!" cried Dr. Bunsen Honeydew.
"I have flicked the last switch. Our Muppet-Lab
Tic-Toc Time Machine is ready to travel. What an
historic moment! And just think–we did it all in the
backstage broom closet!" Beaker meeped weakly.

"Let's go, Beaker! We can visit Pompeii! Atlantis!
The Ice Age! The world, past and future, is ours!
We will zip through eternity!" Beaker peered into the
closet. "Meeeeeeep!" he wailed. He turned and ran in
terror. "Meeeep!" Bunsen would have to catch him
before *he* would zip through eternity.

At that very moment, Kermit was preparing for
the matinée and eating his lunch. He sipped his tea
and then, not looking, put the cup too near the edge
of his desk. SPLOOSH! YUCCH! Tea all over.

"AGH!" cried Kermit. "Beauregard! Help!
Bring some rags and a mop."

He ran to the broom closet.
"Bo! Where are you?" he cried.

"Right here, Kermit.
Want a cupcake?"

"No, I don't want a cupcake!"
said Kermit. "I want your help."

Bo sighed and put the
cupcake back into his lunch bag.
Then he followed Kermit
into the broom closet.

"I can't see anything,"
whispered Kermit.

"That's because it's dark,"
Bo whispered back.

Kermit felt along the wall.
He found a switch and flicked it.
No light came on. The door
slammed shut behind them and
suddenly…the broom closet
chimed, "ZOINK GROING
DING A DING!"

"That's funny," said Kermit.
"I've never heard this broom
closet go 'ZOINK GROING
DING A DING' before."

"CLANG CLANG BUZZ BEEP!"
The walls shook. "KNOCK KNOCK
KNOCK!" Then the noises stopped.

"Gee," said Kermit, "I've never heard it clang and knock before, either."

"It doesn't knock," said Bo. "That's my knees! Uh, I'm scared, Kermit."

"Stay calm, Bo. Find me the flashlight. We'll see what's going on."

Kermit shone the flashlight around the closet. The place was a mess, a dump, a clutter.

"It's nice in here," said Bo.

"Hmm! Those noises must have been the traffic outside," said Kermit. "Anyway, let's clean up the tea."

He picked up a mop, marched out of the broom closet, and smacked right into a tall box that had not been there before.

"Wow! An Egyptian mummy case," he said. "Miss Piggy must have moved her props in for her new number!" The room was filled with marble statues and delicately painted urns.

"Oh no!" Kermit moaned. "She's using a chariot. That'll ruin another stage floor!"

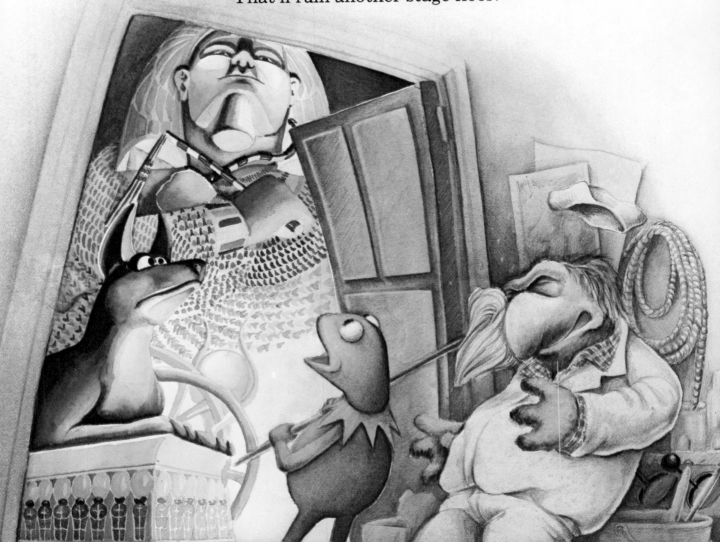

Kermit walked over to a chest of jewels and then
noticed he and Bo were not backstage at all!

"Fozzie?...Scooter?...Anybody?..." he called.
Nobody answered. "Uh-oh, something weird is going on.
Hey, Bo, do you smell incense?"

Bo sniffed the air. "Yeah. Smells like my
Aunt Myrna." His face brightened. "Maybe we're at her
house in Milwaukee!"

"Nice guesswork, Bo, but somehow, I don't think so."

They crept to the end of the room where they found
a mysterious tunnel.

"Uh, after you, Kermit," Bo said.

"Hi, ho..." Kermit gulped. They moved into the darkness.

CHAPTER TWO

Kermit and Bo emerged from the tunnel, blinking in the sunlight.

"We're in the desert!" exclaimed Kermit. "How did we get here?"

"Through the tunnel," answered Bo. How could Kermit have forgotten?

Kermit looked behind him. "YIPES!" he cried. "We just came out of a pyramid."

The truth hit him. "Bo, you and I are in ancient Egypt. Why, we must have gone back in time at least four thousand years! Bunsen! Beaker! The broom closet!!! I TOLD THEM THAT WAS A RIDICULOUS PLACE TO PUT A TIME MACHINE!!!!!"

"Look over there!" Kermit gasped. "Those men are building...the Sphinx!"

Kermit caught his breath and scanned the desert once more. He saw another statue nearby, only this one had no ordinary workers. They were chickens...and they were following a funny-looking creature with a bent nose.

"Don't move, Bo!" said Kermit. "I'd know that nose anywhere!"

Kermit skittered down the sand dune. "Gonzo! What are you doing here?"

"What do you mean, what am I doing here? Who are you?"

"Don't you know me? I'm Kermit."

"Glad to meet you, Kermit. My name's Gonzomosis. I'm a multitalented monument builder. This is my first monument. What do you think?"

"Uh…er…" said Kermit. He stared at Gonzomosis. He sure looks like Gonzo, thought Kermit, but I guess he can't be–this is ancient Egypt. The real Gonzo's back at the Muppet Theater.

"Well, I'd love to chat," said Gonzomosis, "but I can't let those guys with the Sphinx get ahead of me. Okay, girls," he cried, "PUSH!"

The chickens pushed and pushed as hard as they could, but the stone did not budge. "Take five," said Gonzomosis. The chickens collapsed in a tired heap.

"Er, you know," said Kermit, "those Sphinx builders over there have ten thousand slaves helping them."

"Yeah," replied Gonzomosis, "but *I've* got five determined chickens."

Kermit nodded. "True." He started up the sand dune. "Shees," he sighed, "you'd think one Gonzo type was enough."

CHAPTER THREE

KERMIT AND BO ARE LOST IN TIME!
The news traveled swiftly through the Muppet Theater.
"Now, now. Mustn't become alarmed," said Bunsen
in his calmest voice. "Thanks to our advanced
instrumentation, we have calculated all
available data and have scientifically
found Kermit and Bo."
"HOORAY!" the Muppets cheered.
"As far as we can figure," Bunsen
continued, "they're somewhere within
a million years of here."
The cheering stopped.
"Wait…" Robin broke the gloomy silence.
"If Uncle Kermit and Bo are in the past, then they
might be making history, right now. Why don't
we look in our history books for a sign of them?"

"Good thinking, Robin, but
what about the show?" asked Fozzie.
"My fan club is coming today. I can't
break the hearts of those two old ladies."
"That's right," said Scooter.
"Fozzie, you run the show while the
rest of us search for Kermit and Bo."

"Well, I know where *I* shall be." Miss Piggy stepped forward to face the group. "I asked myself, 'Miss Piggy, what would your Kermy expect of you?' And I answered myself, 'Why, he would want you to be Captainette of his search party!'"

The Muppets bowed their heads, touched by her devotion.

She continued. "First, I need a strong and courageous person to travel in this time machine. Who wants to volunteer?"

All heads remained bowed.

"Let me put it this way—who wants to stay here and get clobbered?"

The Muppets piled into the broom closet.

CHAPTER FOUR

Kermit reached the top of the sand dune, his flippers dragging in the hot desert heat.

"Hey, Kermit! I'm wading down here!" yelled Bo.

Ahhh, thought Kermit, a nice cool dip in the Nile! He ran to the bank and splashed into the water. "A few minutes of this and I'll be ready for the trip back home."

"Good," said Bo, " 'cause I'm getting hungry."

"Hungry?! You just ate your lunch!"

"Yeah, but that's in my stomach and my mouth wants a snack. Maybe somebody's having a picnic around here." Bo headed for the shore.

"Stay close," Kermit called. "We're leaving soon."

Then, up the river, a huge barge
floated around the bend. It belonged
to Queen Cleopigtra, Pig of the Nile.

The Queen lay stretched on her silken
couch. She was young and beautiful and
in a very grumpy mood.

"So what if I'm Queen of Egypt?" she said to her high
counselor, Linkus Hogthrobikus. "I'd rather be in love."

"Perhaps your majesty would like to water-ski off the barge?
I'll gladly command the oarsmen to row extra fast," said Linkus,
trying to cheer her up.

Cleopigtra considered his suggestion, then pouted,
"I'd rather sit here and be miserable, thank you."
She sighed and gazed across the Nile.
In the distance, a small, green figure swam against
the river's current. The Queen immediately perked up.

"Oooooh! A froggie!" she squealed, clapping her hands.
Cleopigtra liked the frogs that frolicked on the banks
of the Nile. Then she noticed.
This frog was different....
This frog was special....
This frog...

And then it happened!
BOINGEROINGEROING!!!!
Cleopigtra fell madly in love.

"Stop the boat!" she cried, running
to the rail. "Cease this drift!
My frog has come!"
    Two hairy hands reached down and
yanked Kermit from the water.
    "What the hey?" he exclaimed,
as Sweetumtatum the guard dropped
him on the deck.

Cleopigtra ran to help Kermit up. "Are you all right, Mr....?"
She smiled and batted her eyelashes.

"Kermit."

"Kermit!" she sighed. She leaned closer, batting her
eyelashes so quickly that a light breeze blew into Kermit's face.

"Sure I'm all right. It was only that..."
Kermit looked at Cleopigtra. I don't believe it, he thought.
First, a Gonzo who isn't Gonzo. Now a Miss Piggy who isn't
Miss Piggy.

Then Kermit remembered Bo, all alone in the desert,
looking for a picnic. "I've got to get off!" he said to Cleopigtra.
"I'm in a terrible jam."

Cleopigtra grabbed Kermit's arm. "Wait! Don't you know who I am? I am Queen Cleopigtra, Pig of the Nile. Stay with me and you shall have palaces, servants, jewels, and a magnificent tomb!"

"No thanks," said Kermit.

"You're right," said the Queen. "Who needs that junk? I'm coming with you." She hitched up her robes and swung a leg over the rail.

"You can't come with me!" cried Kermit.

Cleopigtra was crushed. "Oh, I get it. There's someone else, isn't there?"

"No," Kermit explained, "I just have to go alone."

He started to dive when Cleopigtra grabbed his collar.

"I can't let you throw yourself to the wild crocodiles!"

"What?!?" Kermit waved his arms to regain his balance.

"Listen to this." Cleopigtra rummaged through her robes, and from a hidden pocket she pulled out a hair brush, a broken necklace, two stale cinnamon rolls and, finally, a scroll which she unrolled and read to Kermit.

"'The Egyptian Marriage Law:
The Great Gods of Egypt have declared:
A ruler'–that's moi–'may marry anyone.
But any suitor'–that's you–'who turns down a ruler's proposal of marriage shall be thrown to the wild crocodiles.'
Oh, the tragedy of it," sighed Cleopigtra. "My Kermit, a tidbit for a wild beastie." She turned to Kermit. "Do you want that to happen, hmmmmmm?"

"Of course not!" answered Kermit.

"Then we'll have the wedding right here on the barge!" Cleopigtra said.

"Wedding?!?" shouted Kermit. "But..."

Cleopigtra silenced his protests with a big, fat kiss.

Chapter Five

Meanwhile, the time machine would not work with all the Muppets in the closet. Scooter volunteered to travel alone and set off immediately.

Everyone else began flipping through pages in their history books, searching for a sign of Kermit and Bo.

Fozzie ran backstage. "I need another number quick! They're not laughing at my jokes."

"Tell them you're a comic," suggested Waldorf, "that ought to keep 'em laughing."

Fozzie turned to Miss Piggy. "It's the perfect time for your new number. Oh, please! You'd be doing a dying bear a great favor."

"Not until we find Kermit," said Miss Piggy firmly.

Scooter stuck his head out of the broom closet door. "I didn't find Kermit or Bo in the Stone Age," he reported, "but Fozzie, I did find these two juggling cave-men who do a great act with clubs."

"Terrific," said Fozzie. "Let's get them onstage."

CHAPTER SIX

Back on the barge, the royal tailors
fitted Kermit for his kingly wedding robes.

Cleopigtra stood up to make an announcement. "Ahem! As you know, it is ever so important that this wedding reflect the rank and stature of yours truly and her future king, Tutankermit." She gave Kermit a little wave. "So remember, we must carry ourselves with poise, grace and, most especially, dignity." With a toss of her head, the Pig of the Nile turned smartly and…SPLASH!…fell into the Nile.

"QUEEN IN THE SOUP!" The crew and
servants ran about in confusion.

Kermit saw his chance to escape! He threw off
his robes and dove into the water.

"Stop! Kermit! Stop! Blub...ub...blub."
Cleopigtra sank back into the river.

"I've got to find Bo!" said Kermit.
He scrambled up the bank and ran toward the pyramid.
It was so far away!

"Wait! Kermit, my love! I'm coming with you!"
Cleopigtra had reached the shore,
covered in mud.

Kermit quickly ducked into a doorway and crouched
as low as he could.

CLOMP CLOMP CLOMP. The guards ran past his
hiding place. SQUISH SQUISH SQUISH.
Cleopigtra scurried behind them.

"Kermy!" she called in a sad little voice. The sound
of her footsteps faded.

"Hoo boy, now what?" Kermit panted. "If I walk out
on that desert, she'll spot me." Then he had an idea.
"But, I wonder if I could walk *under* the desert.
Sure! I've read that all these Egyptian tombs
have secret tunnels."

He tiptoed down the stairs into the tomb and saw a
bear painting on the wall. The bear turned toward Kermit.

"Great! A visitor!" The bear put down his brush and
hurried over to the frog. "Fozziewozzus is the name.
What's yours?"

"Kermit, and I'm in kind of a rush."

"Hey, Kermit-and-I'm-in-kind-of-a-rush, this won't take
a minute," said the bear. "Not many people come down here to
read my jokes, but listen, someday I'll be famous. Someday,
I'm going to write on the Palace."

Kermit nodded. Now a Fozzie who's not Fozzie, he thought.
A frog could begin to feel at home around here.

They reached the wall that was covered with markings.
"Here, read this," said Fozziewozzus proudly.

Kermit looked blankly at the wall.

"Get it?" the bear asked eagerly.

"Uh, well I can't read your writing," said Kermit.

"I'll tell you what. I'll translate. Knock, knock."

"Who's there?" asked Kermit.

"Egypt."

"Egypt who?"

"Egypt me out of my money. Call the pharaoh patrol."

Fozziewozzus smiled widely and wiggled his ears.
"Funneee, huh?"

"Hysterical," sighed Kermit. "It's just that I don't
feel like laughing."

Kermit told Fozziewozzus about the Muppet
Theater, four thousand years in the future,
about Beauregard who was alone in the desert,
and about Cleopigtra.

"I've got to find Bo and get to that broom
closet. It's the only way we can go home."

Suddenly, Cleopigtra's voice filled the tomb.
"Kermit! I know you're in there!"

"She found me," moaned Kermit.

Fozziewozzus grabbed his hands. "Not yet,
she hasn't!" he said. "Follow me."

CHAPTER SEVEN

Scooter came out of the closet. "Kermit and Bo are not with King Arthur and the Round Table."

The Muppets groaned in disappointment.

Scooter stepped aside and a knight in armor, riding a splendid white stallion, emerged from the closet.

"Terrific!" said Fozzie. "A knight-club act. Get it? …Knight club…?"

No one smiled.

"Well, anyway," shrugged Fozzie, "he's good for five minutes. Then will you do your act, Miss Piggy?"

Miss Piggy shook her head. "When we find Kermy, I'll go on. No sooner!"

"Hey, everybody! I've found them!" cried Robin.
He read from his book: "'Cleopigtra, Pig of the Nile.
2001 B.C. She was not much of a Queen because she
spent all her time inside a pyramid waiting for
a mysterious frog named Kermit.'"

"No ancient hog will get my frog!" yelled
Miss Piggy, running to the broom closet.
Fozzie stood in her path. "You're on next, Miss Piggy.
You said so yourself."

"But Kermy needs me."

"So do we," Scooter reminded her. "Don't worry,
Kermit will understand."

"You're right," said Miss Piggy, running to
her dressing room, "he is a forgiving kind of frog."

Bunsen fiddled with the controls on the time
machine. "All set, Scooter," he said.
"2001 B.C., here we come!"

CHAPTER EIGHT

Cleopigtra left her guards and searched for Kermit by herself. "Kermit?" she whispered as she moved through the tomb.

She bumped into Fozziewozzus. "Have you seen a frog?" she asked the bear.

"Sure, I've seen lots of frogs. They go like this, right?" Fozziewozzus jumped around the room.

"Just what I need," muttered Cleopigtra, "a clown in a bear suit. Forget I asked."

She disappeared into the shadows.

"See," Fozziewozzus said to a mummy along the wall. "I told you I could get rid of her."

"Temporarily," mumbled Kermit. "Now all we need is a secret tunnel to the pyramid."

Fozziewozzus turned and pointed to a large sign.

"Looks like we've found a secret tunnel," he said.

Just then, Fozziewozzus felt someone tap his shoulder.

"Excuse me," said a voice, "is there a snack bar around here?"

"Bo!" cried Kermit.

Beauregard looked at the linen-wrapped frog. "Oh my gosh! I know you. Aren't you The Mummy?"

"No, it's me, Kermit. Come on. I'll explain later."

They ran down the tunnel, and as they rounded a corner, they saw Scooter coming out of the closet.

"Scooter? Scooter? Is that you?" cried Kermit.

"I've found you!" cried Scooter. "Hi, Bo! Hey, Kermit, it's so good to, um, almost see you." Scooter hugged Kermit and slapped him on the back.

"How touching!" Fozziewozzus sniffed, "a boy who loves his mummy." He paused, and his eyes lit up. "Aaaaaaah, that's not bad!"

Kermit turned to the bear. "Thanks for your help, Fozziewozzus. I'd ask you to come with us, but we already have a bear who writes corny jokes."

"I understand. Adding another bear would probably be overBEARing. Get it? OverBEARing? Wocka wocka!" Fozziewozzus gave Kermit's hand a squeeze. "Glad I could help."

Just then, Cleopigtra staggered into the chamber.

"Quick!" cried Kermit. He pulled Bo and Scooter into the closet and slammed the door just in time.

The closet disappeared.

"Kermit!" Cleopigtra ran to where the closet had been. "Didn't you hear me calling? Sweetheart? Frog of my life! Come back with that closet! Don't forget the crocodiles, buster!"

But Kermit, Scooter and Bo were already thousands of years away.

CHAPTER NINE

The Muppets stared at the closet, hoping for the best, but expecting the worst. The door opened slowly. Scooter appeared first. Then Bo. Finally, Kermit stumbled out.

Everyone crowded around Kermit and Bo. "What happened?" they all shouted. Suddenly, a familiar voice echoed backstage.

"Oh, Kermy! I knew we could never be parted!"

Kermit looked up to see Cleopigtra running down the stairs!

For one shocked moment, he forgot where he was. "Oh, no!" he cried, as she swept him into her bejeweled arms. "How did you find me?"

"Oh, Kermy, I was so worried. Did you miss me?" asked Miss Piggy.

Kermit returned to his senses. "Well, Miss Piggy," he said slowly, "it seems as if I've never been away from you." And Miss Piggy, ready to go on stage for her sensational new Egyptian number, gave Kermit a big, fat kiss.

Kermit was glad to be home.